ROCK & ROLL
HALL OF FAMERS

Ray Charles

MARK BEYER

the rosen publishing group's
rosen central

To Brother Ray—Thanks for the music

Published in 2003 by The Rosen Publishing Group, Inc.
29 East 21st Street, New York, NY 10010

First Edition

Library of Congress Cataloging-in-Publication Data

Beyer, Mark (Mark T.)
Ray Charles / by Mark Beyer.– 1st ed.
    p. cm. — (Rock & roll hall of famers)
Includes discography (p.   ), bibliographical references (p.   ), and index.
Summary: Traces the personal life and musical career of the blind singer, musician, and composer, Ray Charles.
ISBN 0-8239-3642-2 (lib. bdg.)
1. Charles, Ray, 1930– —Juvenile literature. 2. Singers—United States—Biography—Juvenile literature. [1. Charles, Ray, 1930–
2. Singers. 3. African Americans—Biography.
4. Blind. 5. People with disabilities.] I. Title. II. Series.
ML3930.C443 B49 2002
782.42164'092—dc21

                                                                    2001008220

Manufactured in the United States of America

CONTENTS

Introduction   5

1. A Southern Childhood   7

2. Early Travels and Gigs   26

3. Breakthrough Stardom   44

4. Ups and Downs   58

5. The 1980s Comeback   82

6. On Cruise Control   96

Selected Discography   103

Glossary   104

To Find Out More   106

For Further Reading   108

Index   109

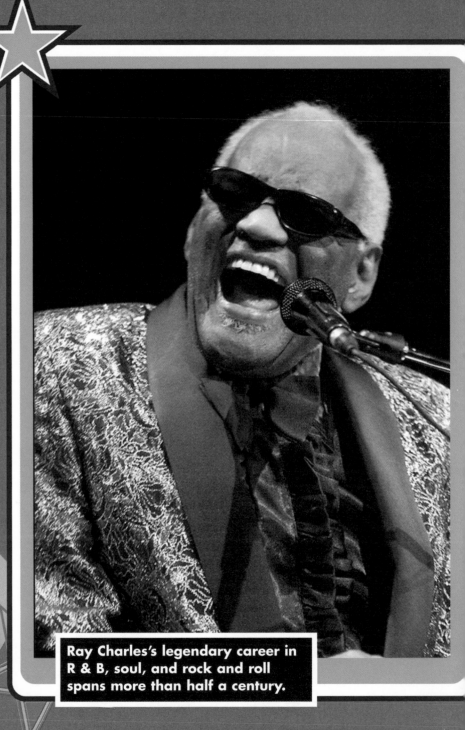

Ray Charles's legendary career in R & B, soul, and rock and roll spans more than half a century.

Introduction

All careers have high and low points. A career reflects life, and a music career has the advantage of combining life with art. Ray Charles has lived the highs and felt the lows in his sixty-plus-year (and going strong!) career. The advantages of his natural musical talents were never harmed by the fact that he was blind. Ray adjusted to any difficulty he faced. The man known today as Brother Ray never lets hurdles keep him from his goals.

"I was born with music inside me," Ray has said.

"That's the only explanation I know of, since none of my relatives could sing or play an instrument. Music was one of my parts, like my liver, my kidneys, my heart. Like my blood."

Ray Charles started playing music at the age of three. Today, Ray is known for the innovation he brought to the blues, jazz, pop, country and western, and R & B. He has recorded more than sixty-five albums. Many of his 600 songs are known to each of us. We hum them and hear them in commercials, or we listen to other recording artists sing their versions of his classics. These endearing sounds are all gifts from Brother Ray.

A Southern Childhood

In 1930, Albany, Georgia, was a sleepy southern farm town. It was hot and dusty, and many families struggled financially. That year, Raymond Charles Robinson was born on September 23. His mother, Aretha Williams, was a small woman, weighing a little over a hundred pounds. She had only a fifth-grade education but worked hard to care for her children. Everyone called her Retha.

Bailey Robinson, Ray's father, worked on the railroads at the time. Ray doesn't know for sure if his mother and father were ever married to each other, but he believes they weren't. At the time of Ray's birth, Bailey was married to a woman named Mary Jane. In his autobiography, *Brother Ray*, Ray wrote that he believes Bailey and Retha had an affair. It was that affair that brought Ray into the world.

Family Life

Shortly after Ray's birth, Retha and Ray moved to Greenville, Florida. Greenville was just across the Georgia border. It was another backwoods town. Most of its citizens worked in its sawmill. The townspeople called the town "Greensville." Ray always thought of his hometown as "Greensville," with an *s*.

A year after Ray was born, his brother, George, was born. This is as far as the Robinson family grew, though. As far back as Ray can remember, his father, Bailey, was never a part of his life. In Greenville, Bailey lived with Mary Jane. Regardless of his father's lack of interest, though, Ray remembers Retha and Mary Jane caring for him as if he had two mothers. In fact, Mary Jane and Retha were friendly, if not friends. Ray called Retha "Mama" and Mary Jane "Mother."

Retha supported her two boys by washing and ironing for the white families living in Greenville. Mary Jane was a big woman who worked with the men in the sawmill. Ray was too young to remember all the specifics of his mother and father's (and Mary Jane's) relationship. He does remember that they all loved him and his brother, though.

His Mother's Son

There was no doubt who raised Ray: Retha. "Mama was a rare human being," Ray wrote in *Brother Ray*. "She was no softy; really strict as hell. I mean discipline was her middle name." Retha was a strong woman at heart. She knew it was her job to raise her two boys right. She didn't drink or smoke. She took her boys to church each week, but that was all. She worked too hard to be dragging them to church more than she thought was necessary.

As Ray remembers his childhood, his family was poorer than most. That didn't faze Retha, though. She taught her boys to respect

Ray Charles, pictured here at the piano in 1960, first started playing at the age of three.

themselves. There would be no begging in her family. And her boys were not to steal. These were the most important rules of the house. Ray learned them quickly.

Other than strict rules and lots of chores, Ray was a typical boy. He was nice, clean, and courteous; he was also wild and full of energy. He and George liked to go into the woods and run around. They played in the wild berry patches until their mother called them home. They were also country boys who knew the lessons of survival. Ray remembers watching hogs being slaughtered for the family's evening meal. This was, of course, before he was blind.

A Bright, Musical World

Ray Charles was not born blind. It was a few more years before Ray lost his eyesight. At three years old, he was absorbing the bright world as any other three-year-old did. Ray remembers playing in the pine forests. He remembers the pecans from the trees in Greenville. He also remembers those pigs, cows, and chickens from his youth.

Greenville had cafes and diners, and one that Ray kept going back to was the Red Wing Cafe. Ray was fascinated with the Red Wing because it had a piano. When Ray heard the owner, Wylie Pitman, play that piano, he had to go listen. Ray was only three, but he walked right up to the piano and Mr. Pit (as Ray soon

11

called him) took notice. Ray felt the music in his bones. He felt the rhythm of the notes and knew they were right. He understood that music was a part of him.

Mr. Pit took to Ray quickly. Ray thinks it's because Mr. Pit and his wife, Miss Georgia, didn't have kids of their own. Either way, Ray showed interest in playing the piano, and Mr. Pit took him up on his knee and let him run his fingers over the keys. "That was a good feeling," Ray recalls. Soon, Mr. Pit let Ray play the piano as much as Ray could. Making music out of all those individual sounds fascinated Ray. Even today he's still hooked on the mechanics of music—putting notes together to make sound that is beautiful.

Mr. Pit was Ray's first and biggest musical influence. Mr. Pit played boogie-woogie piano. This was a fast blues style popular in the South at the time. It was a style the best players of the day used to get a crowd loose and happy. Along with jazz, boogie-woogie is what Ray heard first and most often from age three until he went away to a school for the blind at age seven.

The Red Wing Cafe also had a jukebox, which, if Mr. Pit wasn't playing the piano, was lit up and kicking out boogie-woogie, jazz, and the big bands of the day. Ray sat on a bench in the Red Wing that rested against the jukebox speaker. He listened for hours to the best blues artists of the day: Pete Johnson, Tampa Red, Blind Boy Phillips, Meade Lux Lewis, Albert Ammons, and Washboard Sam.

At the same time, Ray was given his first nicknames. The first was "Mechanic" for how much he loved to tinker with engines. The other was "RC," the first letters of his first and middle names, Ray Charles. For the next couple of years, Ray learned to play on the piano, listened to the jukebox, and got a few lickings from his mother for doing typical mischievous kid stuff.

Brother George

When Ray was five years old, he experienced his first brush with tragedy. Ray and his four-year-old brother, George, were playing in the backyard on a summer day. Inside the house, Retha was washing clothes. A huge tub of water sat in the yard. Ray watched George climb into the tub. They had always liked to swim and splash in the tub. George splashed and swam until Ray didn't hear his little brother anymore. He ran to the tub and found George drowning in the water. Ray tried to pull George out of the tub, but he didn't have the strength. He ran inside screaming for his mother to come help. Retha followed Ray outside and pulled George from the tub. Retha tried to pump the water out of George's lungs. She tried to breathe air into him. After a few minutes, she stopped. George was dead. Retha sat above George, crying. Ray stood a few feet away, stunned. Today, Ray barely remembers the funeral or his brother's burial. Oddly, those images were some of the last he would ever see. Over the next few months, his vision was lost.

Blindness

The country doctors didn't know why Ray was losing his sight. They knew only that there was no hope. From the time Ray was five until he

A reflective Ray Charles plays the piano during a gig in 1964.

was seven, his sight melted away. First he lost the ability to see clear shapes. Then color began to go. He woke each morning with mucus caked around his eyes. Aretha used washcloths soaked with warm water to wipe Ray's eyes. No one knew how or why, but Ray was going blind.

Retha received counseling and advice about what to do with Ray. Some people suggested that Ray be sent to the State School for the Blind in St. Augustine, Florida. Retha soon realized this would be the best thing for Ray. She didn't want to send her boy away, but what else could she do? There was no one in Greenville that could help a blind boy learn. And Retha knew that Ray would need to learn a lot more than just what was written in books in order to get by. She knew, and would soon tell Ray, that she would not be able to watch out for him for the rest of his life.

Meanwhile, Retha wasn't babying Ray, either. He still had his chores to do at home. Nearly blind as he was, Ray still had legs, arms, and a brain. Retha knew he could figure out how to wash the floor, make his bed, sweep the porch, and even chop wood. Chop wood? A blind child? Yes! Retha sent Ray out back with a hatchet to chop wood for the kitchen stove. Her neighbors had a fit. How could Retha put a hatchet into the hands of a blind boy? Ray recalls what Retha told them: "'He's blind,' Mama told them, 'but he ain't stupid.'"

Retha's confidence in her son gave Ray his own sense of confidence. He didn't stay at home and feel sorry for himself. He went outside, played with the other kids, and went into town. He learned how to get around and do things by himself.

The School for the Blind

A few weeks before he turned seven, Retha put Ray on a train to St. Augustine. This was September 1937, and the State School for the Blind was 160 miles away. This was a long way for a blind boy to travel alone. They had no choice, though. Retha couldn't afford to go with him.

Ray cried most of the way there. Kids on the train teased him. When he got to the school in St. Augustine, Ray realized he needed to adapt. This was not going to be the first change in his life. He quickly got into the routine of school and classes, and began to make friends.

Ray's first year at the school was filled with learning how to read braille. Braille is a reading system of raised dots on a page. Each series of dots is equal to a letter of the alphabet. When accustomed to braille, blind people are able to read nearly as quickly as sighted people. Ray learned braille quickly, and then he began to read. He wasn't a book-learning kind of person, though. He liked to do things with his hands.

By the time Ray was ten, he was working in the woodshop at school. He learned how to make crafts. He enjoyed making brooms and mops. He was an especially good weaver and made chair bottoms from cane.

There was also plenty of playtime at the school. Ray liked to run in the schoolyard. The kids had races, and Ray often won. By this time, Ray was completely blind. Still, he didn't let his blindness stop him from enjoying a normal childhood like everyone else.

Musical Ambitions

The State School for the Blind had a music department. Ray now had the chance to study music formally. His teachers taught him to play classical music. Ray learned Mozart, Beethoven, Strauss, and Chopin. Ray sometimes broke away and played his boogie-woogie, but the teachers didn't like that much. Nonetheless, Ray was learning much more about the piano and music than he had in the years playing with Mr. Pit at the Red Wing Cafe. He began to understand how music was put together. He appreciated learning the classical pieces, though they weren't what he really liked to play.

Ray knew that the three music teachers he had at school liked the blues. They were there, however, to teach what was thought to be proper music. There were three pianos at the school, and Ray tried to play on the one in the boy's section as much as possible. He also wasn't the only musician at the school. As Ray remembers it, there were several boys who could really play the piano. They played boogie-woogie like he'd heard on the jukebox! They were older than he was, and Ray admired their work. He realized that they were copying the styles of the best players around. Ray had been doing this, too, but now he was better and so he began to imitate the best of the best.

Meanwhile, Ray was getting out and exploring St. Augustine. He learned how to get around the city as easily as he had Greenville. His trick was this: To cross a street, he waited for a group of ladies who were also crossing. When he heard them start off the curb, Ray would walk with them and get to the other side.

Ray also asked questions. If he wanted to get something to eat, he asked someone where a diner was. If he needed to take a bus, he'd ask someone where the bus stop was. Ray was becoming independent. He knew that the only way he would make it in life was to do things for himself. Still, he understood that he'd have to have some help, but those times would not keep him from living life to the fullest.

Did You Know?

Blind people have a heightened sense of sound, smell, and touch. They rely on these other senses to make up for the loss of their sight. As a boy, Ray Charles used sound to help him tell where people were in a room. He could also tell how far away from a building he was by the echo sounds made off walls. The sounds around Ray Charles taught him how to function in a sightless world.

A Painful Tragedy

In May 1945, Ray was fifteen years old. He was playing the piano at school and getting jobs playing in clubs at night in St. Augustine. He had become well known and likable because of his playing style. He was able to play any kind of music for any type of crowd. This gave him

an opportunity to make money. And so he did.
He knew people around town, and they knew
other people who could use a pianist like Ray.

One day, though, Ray's fingers stopped
playing and didn't start again for many months:
The school officials had called Ray into an office
and told him his mother had died. Ray was
dumbstruck. "Nothing had ever hit me like that,"
he remembers. "Mama had raised me, and now
she was gone. I couldn't deal with that. And for a
while, I went a little crazy."

Ray returned to Greenville for Retha's funeral.
And then he just sat in pain at home. He
couldn't eat, hardly slept, and began to get
physically ill. Nothing anyone said to him made a
difference. Mary Jane cared for him. Mr. Pit and
Miss Georgia were also very kind. A doctor told
Ray that Retha had died in her sleep. She had
died of a heart attack. Retha was only thirty-two
years old. But she was dead.

After a week of being really down, friends
called in Ma Beck. Ma Beck was an old matriarch
of the black section of Greenville. Ma Beck had
twenty-two children and was very wise about life,

death, love, and sickness. She came to Ray and told him all the things about Retha that Ray knew were true. Retha had taught him to be strong, to be caring, to look ahead in life, and not to let the worst of life get him down. Ray suddenly realized that Ma Beck was absolutely right. Ray went to the funeral and said good-bye to his mother. He touched her one last time; he ran his hand over her face.

For weeks afterward, Ray stayed in Greenville. He was determined to do what his mother had taught him to do. He wasn't going to beg. He wasn't going to steal. He was going to be a good, hardworking man and work for his way in the world. When Ray finally came to a decision, it was one that would change his life. He was going to go on the road, alone, and be a musician.

Ray Charles

1930
Ray Charles Robinson is born on September 23 to Aretha Williams.

1945
Aretha Williams dies; Ray goes on the road as a musician at age fifteen.

1952
Atlantic Records signs Ray to his first three-year contract.

1936
Ray loses his eyesight; many years later, some doctors suggest it was caused by glaucoma.

1949
Ray's first song, "Confession Blues," is recorded.

1955
Ray marries Della Bea Howard on April 5; on May 25, Ray Jr. is born.

1960
Ray changes record labels and signs with ABC; *Genius Hits the Road* is released, with "Georgia on My Mind" going up to number one on the charts.

1984
Ray releases the country and western album *Friendship* through Columbia Records. It soars to number one.

1993
Ray sings "America the Beautiful" at President Bill Clinton's inaugural ball.

1969
Ray leaves ABC Records to have his own label, Tangerine, put out his albums.

1990
Ray begins a two-year series of Pepsi-Cola television commercials; a younger audience begins to like his music.

Early Travels and Gigs

2

Ray was going on the road alone. This didn't mean he wouldn't look for or accept a little help from people. Having friends of the family living in Jacksonville, Florida, made it easier for Ray to leave Greenville and the State School for the Blind. His father's wife, Mary Jane, had a close friend, Louise. Louise lived with her sister Lena Mae and her brother-in-law, Fred Thompson. They owned a house in downtown Jacksonville. They accepted Ray without question. This situation was ideal because Ray had freedom, but he also had elders to look out for him.

Life with the Thompsons

The family liked having Ray around. He was kind, considerate, and offered respect to his hosts. The Thompsons gave Ray his own room and the bounty of their kitchen. Ray offered to pay for food, but the Thompsons wouldn't hear of it. Nonetheless, Ray would often bring home a bag of groceries and leave it in the kitchen as payment.

The Thompsons allowed Ray to use their home as if it were his own, but they were not about to let Ray use their house as a bachelor pad. He was just sixteen years old, but if he was going to work for a living, he had to act like an adult. Ray had to be home at a certain time each evening. If he was going to be late, he had to call. This life was not unlike any teenager's in the 1990s and 2000s! Ray understood these rules, and he used them to keep himself in line, too.

Did You Know?

Ray refused to use a cane or get a Seeing Eye dog to help him get around. His independent-mindedness would not allow him to be led around by an animal. He also didn't want to look foolish tapping walls with a cane. Ray also refused to ever play the guitar. He believed that a guitar in a blind man's hands was a pitiful sight and made the man look like a beggar.

Learning the Ropes

Ray felt in his heart that music was what he should do in life. He immediately set out in Jacksonville to find work playing piano. This was late 1945. World War II (1938–1945) had just ended that same year. Men were coming home. More women were working than ever before. People needed places to go to entertain themselves at night and on the weekends. That meant there were plenty of bars and clubs, and plenty of musicians were needed to play music.

Ray walked around Jacksonville and listened for the sound of pianos outside bars and restaurants. When he heard one, he'd go in and listen. He began to meet people—the right people. Ray was not shy about talking to anybody about his piano playing. He knew he was good and only needed one chance for a band or club owner to hear him play. Soon musicians and club owners and people in the bars hooked Ray up with bands. He joined the musicians union. The union helped Ray find work and helped him if there was ever a problem with a band, club, or manager. For that he paid a small part of his nightly pay.

Early gigs saw Ray sitting in on the piano when a band's regular player was out sick or had left the band. Ray was a fast learner. He picked up rhythms and learned songs so quickly that bands knew he was reliable. He was still a kid, though, and some people doubted his talent if they hadn't yet heard him play: Ray

Ray Charles performs at McCormick Place, a major music venue in Chicago, Illinois, in 1961.

would tell them, "Say, man, I'll play, and if you don't like it, don't pay me." His trust in people, and his faith in himself, always got them to pay him something.

The Scuttlebutt

Playing so many small gigs gave Ray the reputation of a person who could play anything! Each kind of music—jazz, blues, boogie-woogie, country—had its own rhythm and beat. Moving from one kind of music to another was difficult for most musicians. Being able to do it with such excellence made Ray a musician in demand. Sure, sometimes he didn't have a gig for days, but more often than not he was playing piano in a cafe or club until late at night.

The first big band Ray played with was Henry Washington's sixteen-piece orchestra. They played Count Basie and Billy Eckstine styles: something that had a beat but that wasn't wild like a barroom's nasty blues. Again, Ray wasn't the regular pianist, but he was learning how to work with different people. He was learning more styles.

More important, he was learning what the different white and black crowds liked to listen to. He realized that most bands played the styles and songs of the hottest names in the music world.

Ray had already experimented with imitating artists. He was well known for his Nat King Cole voice impersonations. People told Ray they couldn't tell the two apart if their eyes were closed. Cole was a favorite with the white audiences because he had such a smooth, polished style. Charles Brown was another pianist whose voice Ray impersonated. Brown, like Cole, was a romantic crooner. Ray's ability to mimic both their voices and styles gave him the opportunity to play to white audiences. This was where the real money was.

On a good night, Ray's Nat King Cole impersonation could get him several five-dollar tips. This was good money to Ray. It was a time when Ray learned some valuable lessons. He knew that if he could play all musical styles, he'd never go hungry. By the time he left Jacksonville a year later, Ray could easily blend into any band: blues, swing, jazz, boogie, even hillbilly!

Ray Charles plays around with child actor Piers Bishop in May 1964.

Social Life

Listening to the radio was still Ray's favorite way to relax. The Thompsons liked to listen to the *Grand Ole Opry.* Ray also got hooked on the radio series, as well as *The Shadow, Jack Armstrong,* and *Amos 'n' Andy.*

The Thompsons didn't own a piano. They did have friends who owned them, though. Ray liked to be asked to spend an evening out at a neighbor's, playing the piano. But he couldn't just sit at the keyboard and practice any time he wanted or improvise. Improvisation is what he really needed to find his own style, his own voice. He had far too little opportunity for that in his first few years. When he played at a neighbor's house, he played the songs they wanted to hear. Cole, Basie, Armstrong, and classical tunes were second nature to Ray now. His soul was made to play blues and jazz. The musicians he looked up to were men like Tampa Red, Washboard Sam, Big Boy Crudup, and Muddy Waters. They were where music was at in 1946.

At seventeen, Ray was no longer shy around women. He'd been playing piano in clubs and at social events for nearly five years. He'd had plenty of time to meet girls. Though Ray didn't find enough time to form lasting relationships, he had many girlfriends. His first in Jacksonville was a girl named Lovie Herman. Her parents owned a piano, and Ray could be found entertaining Lovie a lot. They got to know each other well, but Ray's true love at this time was music. Little did any woman he'd ever know realize that would never change.

Orlando

In late 1946, Ray got an offer to play some gigs in Orlando. A man named Tiny York had a band that played a lot of out-of-town gigs. Ray liked to play as often as possible. When Tiny offered him a series of gigs in Orlando, Ray jumped at the chance. Ray was not in a position to pass up work.

Unfortunately, once the band got to Orlando, the gigs didn't happen as Tiny had planned. He thought Ray's Cole and Brown imitations would be a hit. Other band members had some of their own imitations going, too. But the gigs just never appeared. Ray was stranded. There was no real reason for Ray to run back to Jacksonville, though. Ray had already been thinking about leaving. He decided to give Orlando a shot on his own.

The next year turned out to be the hardest in Ray's life. There was little happening musically in Orlando. Ray was virtually unknown, even though he'd been a real pro back in Jacksonville. He was learning a valuable lesson about road life and making oneself known everywhere. Ray sometimes had to go a couple of days without food. He was paying $3 a week for a room. Sometimes he barely had the money.

Even though Ray was nearly flat broke, he didn't let himself go. His mother had taught him to always be clean and courteous. Ray owned a couple of shirts, pants, and socks and underwear. He made sure he looked good each night he went out looking for work.

One night, Ray wandered into the Sunshine Club. He'd been there before. Joe Anderson was a tenor sax player who ran the house band. He'd heard Ray play and liked his style. Anderson began to use Ray whenever he could. Then something even better happened. Anderson learned that Ray also wrote music. Anderson's band had been playing music written by other outside musicians. When

Anderson offered Ray a chance to write for the band, it was an easy decision for the young man now known as RC.

Ray writes music one note at a time. He dictates his notes to someone who copies them onto a musical score sheet. Ray doesn't sit at the piano and play with the keys to find the rhythm. Ray already has this in his head. He hears the song in his mind and calls the notes out as he hears them. When the score is put on paper, Ray works at the arrangement. Arrangements tell which instruments play at what time in the piece. They dictate how loud or soft a musician needs to play each measure, or string of notes. Ray, of course, didn't read sheet music. He had everything memorized.

Unfortunately, Ray didn't think to ask to get paid for his extra work with the band. He was happy to be playing. And writing? Well, that was gravy. Years later he wrote in his autobiography that he didn't blame Anderson for not offering more money. It was business, and each person had to take care of himself. This was another lesson Ray learned early.

Tampa

After a year in Orlando, Ray grew restless. There were a lot of great musicians roaming the South in the late 1940s. When competition took food money out of his hands, Ray knew it was time for a change.

Tampa was an important southern port town after WWII. People from all across the South and the Caribbean used Tampa as their source of income. Ray saw great potential for himself there. Nevertheless, he rolled into Tampa with little money. He was no longer an untested

Fun Fact!

Ray always asked to get paid in single dollar bills. That way he knew he could never get cheated out of the proper pay.

Ray Charles created a signature style of soloing on the piano while singing along.

musician, though. He soon ran into other musicians he'd known from around Florida.

A guitar player named Gosady McGee introduced Ray to two sisters in town. Freddie and Lydia liked Ray right off and offered to let him stay at their house. When Ray arrived, he found out the ladies owned a piano. He had never had free use of a piano before. He took advantage of this opportunity and began to practice many hours every day.

Luck ran his way in getting work quickly, too. He started playing piano for Charlie Brantley's seven-piece band. They played blues, jazz, swing, and just about anything else halls and clubs wanted them to play. Ray made himself a hit in the band with his Cole and Brown imitations. The band traveled to nearby cities such as Ocala and Sarasota. Ray spent his daytime hours traveling by car to gigs and playing in bars until after midnight.

Bands came and went, though, and so did Ray. In 1948, Ray played piano for an all-white hillbilly band called the Florida Playboys. They played country and western joints. Ray didn't care. The band paid good money. And it didn't matter to Ray that the band was all white. He couldn't see them to care either way.

First Recordings

With the good money he earned playing hillbilly songs, Ray bought a wire recorder, a device that could record songs for Ray. He set it up in the living room at Freddie and Lydia's. He and some musicians jammed in the room while the recorder was going. One day they recorded a song Ray had written. "I Found My Baby There" sounded distant and tinny on playback, but Ray was pleased with the playing. During the song, Ray played a piano solo and began to hum the notes as he played. Later, he realized that he'd never heard this done before. Ray was beginning to create his own style.

The Love Bug

Ray dated plenty of women in Tampa. One night, though, he met Louise Mitchell. Ray and Louise dated and eventually fell in love. Ray found that he wanted to be with Louise all the time.

Louise's parents had a lot of problems with the teens' relationship, though. First off, Ray was blind. Second, he was a musician. They didn't see much of a future for their daughter dating—and maybe marrying—a blind musician. The conflict between Louise and her parents just made her and Ray closer.

One day the couple got fed up with the harassment Louise was getting from her parents. Ray suggested they run off to Miami. They did, moving into a room in a house and passing themselves off as a married couple. Soon, though, the cat was out of the bag, and the Mitchells called their daughter from Tampa.

After only a few weeks, the teens went back to Tampa. It didn't take long before Ray grew restless again. He wanted to experience more of the world.

3

Breakthrough Stardom

The question this time was where Ray should go. He wasn't ready yet for Chicago, New Orleans, Los Angeles, or New York. He felt those cities were too big. He'd heard that the West Coast was as hopping with musicians as Florida was. He chose Seattle because it was the furthest little big city from Tampa. He promised Louise he'd send a ticket for her once he got settled.

A Year in Seattle

The train trip to Seattle took five days. Ray had barely enough money to make it. He didn't realize the train didn't drive straight through. It stopped at night, and so passengers had to find a place to stay. Ray got some help from the travelers' bureau. They helped him locate cheap rooms close to the station each night.

The year was 1948, and Ray was starting over again. This didn't scare him, though. He'd done it all before. Luck would serve him again. The very night he came to Seattle, he wandered into a club that he'd heard served food until late. Ray was hungry, but then he heard that a talent show was going on.

The owner almost didn't let Ray in the club. He looked too young! But Ray talked him into letting him play. When Ray took the stage, he played from the heart. The crowd loved him. He sang Charles Brown's "Traveling Blues" and "Drifting Blues." Afterward, a man asked him if he could get a band together for some gigs at the Elks Club. Ray went to the musicians' union the next day.

A few months later, Gosady McGee went to Seattle. He and Ray put together a new trio. Gosady was on guitar, Milt Garred played bass, and Ray was up front singing and playing piano. They called themselves the McSon Trio, taken from the "Mc" in McGee and "Son" in Ray's last name, Robinson. Ray's popularity started to rise, but there was already another celebrity named Ray Robinson—the great Sugar Ray Robinson, to be exact. Ray thought this would be a good time to make himself distinct. He began to go by the name Ray Charles.

First Record

The McSon Trio played everywhere in and near Seattle. Soon they got a gig to play on a local radio station, KRSC. Soon after, a record label owner approached Ray to record a single. Ray knew that he'd just made it as a musician.

Jack Lauderdale owned Downbeat Records. The McSon Trio recorded Ray's "Confession Blues." It was an old song he'd written back in Florida. Over the next few months, the band recorded more songs down in Los Angeles. Ray did his L.A. recordings without his band. He got to play with some heavy hitters, like Johnny Miller and the brothers Oscar and Johnny Moore. Ray's first national hit, "Baby, Let Me Hold Your Hand," came out of these recording sessions.

The Split with Louise

Ray had kept his promise to bring Louise to Seattle. She arrived only a month after Ray. They lived happily together for a while, but then Ray felt smothered. He saw that he had a lot more responsibility than he really wanted. Also, Louise's parents were still bothering her to drop Ray.

They often fought, but just as often quickly made up. After one such fight, though, Louise called her mother. Mrs. Mitchell demanded that Ray come to the phone. She told him to send Louise back to Tampa. Ray refused, but then he told Mrs. Mitchell that if she sent a ticket, Ray would put Louise on a train.

Ray and Louise made up from this fight, too. But a few weeks later, a letter came to their

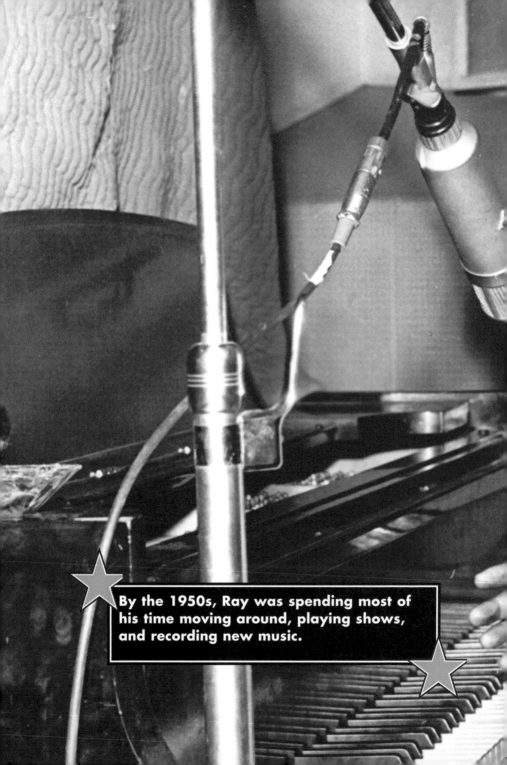

By the 1950s, Ray was spending most of his time moving around, playing shows, and recording new music.

house with a train ticket for Tampa. Ray was in a spot. He'd promised Mrs. Mitchell he'd send Louise back if a ticket came for her. He decided he couldn't go back on his word. Besides, the relationship had almost run its course. In 1949, Louise went back to Tampa for good.

Meanwhile, Jack Lauderdale wanted the McSon Trio to record more records. It was a good time for Ray to leave Seattle.

Los Angeles and Atlantic Records

Ray moved to Los Angeles in 1950. The music recording industry was growing larger than ever. Big names like Charlie Parker and Dizzy Gillespie topped the black artist charts. Bebop was all the craze, too. Ray loved to play this light, powerful, rhythmic dance music. The McSon Trio played in many dance halls.

Meanwhile, Louise learned that she was pregnant. Ray was on the road and wouldn't find out for months. His daughter, Evelyn, was born in Tampa. Ray wanted to do the right thing and began sending money regularly to Louise. In later years, he would always help Evelyn with any financial needs.

Back in L.A., Ray's band recorded more of his own material. Singing like Nat King Cole and Charles Brown came sort of natural to Ray. But it was also hard work. Ray had to prepare his voice and throat to hit their vocal levels. One day, Ray sang using his own voice. He really liked what he heard. So did Jack Lauderdale. For a while now, Jack had been more interested in Ray's talents than the complete band. After only two years, the band broke up. Ray was about to get the chance of a lifetime.

Lauderdale hooked Ray up with a hot big band that had a traveling show. Lowell Fulson's blues band would be a great chance to showcase Ray's talents. Ray went on the road with Fulson's band and played piano. In the middle of the long set, Ray was given three solo songs with the band as backup. Fulson always finished the show.

Fulson especially liked Ray because he was able to take control of the band. Ray was a songwriter and arranger. Since he knew how

By the early 1950s, Ray was ready to truly establish himself as a bandleader and composer.

to put the sounds together to make them kick, he was the natural choice to get the band in shape. For the next eighteen months, the band did gigs up and down the California coast. The pay was good, but still Ray wasn't getting anything extra for his writing and arranging. He knew that would have to change.

While on the road, Ray met a woman named Eileen Williams in Columbus, Ohio. She was a beautician, and the two seemed to fall in love overnight. In fact, after three weeks, they decided to get married. This was a poor choice, as they both quickly found out. Ray was never around, and when he was, he complained that Eileen drank too much. The marriage lasted about a year.

Ray had watched several musicians make it on their own. He wanted to do the same. He wanted to write and record his own songs, be his own band leader, and be his own boss. He quit Fulson's band and hired a woman taxi driver he'd met in New Orleans to drive him around the country. He signed with the Billy Shaw Agency in New York. They managed him and supplied him with gigs. Another year on the road saw Ray build his reputation as a consummate singer, songwriter, and hot talent. Newly established Atlantic Records wanted to sign a guy such as Ray. He had star quality in his voice, music, and onstage charisma. In 1952, Ray signed a contract with Atlantic to record with them.

Ray's early Atlantic records featured some songs he'd written and some he got from others. "The Sun's Gonna Shine Again" was his first recording for Atlantic. Ray would record for Atlantic for the next seven years.

A New Band

Ray had achieved popularity as a single musician. But he knew that adding a band to play his music, expanding it with horn and rhythm sections, and laying down drum tracks would push him over the top. His chance at having his own band came in 1954, the year that he put together a seven-piece band. David "Fathead" Newman played baritone sax.

A.D. Norris played tenor sax. Clanky
White and Joe Bridgewater played trumpet.
Johnny Bell played bass, and Bill Peoples kept
the beat on drums. Ray was up front, singing
and playing the keys.

Ray wrote the songs, arranged the music,
and kept the band playing at their best. He
even produced all the band's records for
Atlantic, even though he was only twenty-three
at the time. It was an unprecedented feat for
someone so young. Ahmet Ertegun, Atlantic
Record's president, allowed it to happen
because he knew that Ray could do it better
than anyone.

Ray was now making enough money to buy
two cars for the band. A Ford and a DeSoto
station wagon carried the seven musicians and
their instruments all over the country. They drove
all day to get to gigs at night. Few musicians of
the day had any other choice.

In 1955, the band added three women as
backup singers. Ray liked how their voices
contrasted with his own. They harmonized songs
in such a way that Ray would from that day

By 1954, Ray Charles had finally assembled a real band that would help him deliver hit song after hit song.

forward always have the Raeletts. The band was now eleven strong.

A year later the band recorded "I Got a Woman." It became a huge hit. Ray's band was a whopping success. For the next forty-six years, Ray would have a band around him to sing his tunes his way. He'd finally made it!

Ups and Downs

In the late 1950s Ray blended jazz and gospel to form the Ray Charles sound. He played everything else, of course, but kept coming back to the spiritual side that music gave to his idea of songwriting. Ray wrote songs about everyday problems, feelings, and joys.

Rock and roll had burst onto the music world in 1955. Ray didn't change with it. He used what suited his style and left the rest to the kids coming up. Black artists like Chuck Berry, Little Richard, and Fats Domino sold millions of records to a new, white audience. Ray was different and would always remain different. He wrote serious songs with a lot of feeling. He wasn't about to change for the industry.

Marriage

In 1955, Ray married a woman named Della Bea Howard, from Houston, Texas. Ray met Della Bea in 1954 after she had heard him interviewed on the radio in Houston and called the station. Ray had complimented the Cecil Shaw Singers, and Della Bea was part of that group. The two hit it off quickly. They soon married, and Della Bea lived in Dallas while Ray toured.

In May 1955, Ray Jr. was born. Ray was terrified of hurting his son, Ray Jr., because he was so little. After a while, though, Ray enjoyed being a father, although he still spent most of his time on the road touring. He had to make money to support his family now. The money was much better these days. Still, Ray was a musician, and musicians made their money when they played for audiences.

Ray and Della Bea would have two more children. David was born in 1958, and Robert was born two years after that. Ray's constant infidelities produced four more children from four different women around the United States. He suffered through as many legal battles from these women, who sued Ray for child support. In each case he lost. Della Bea was hurt by all of these sad moments in their marriage.

Ray and Della Bea's marriage lasted twenty-one years. Ray blames their breakup on the same things as all his other relationships. The pressure of working so much and being around too little were relationship killers. In interviews, Ray never mentioned his affairs with other women as the cause of his divorce.

Drug Bust

Ray had been smoking marijuana and shooting heroin since his Seattle days. He claims that he was never a junkie, although it was often reported otherwise in newspapers. He says he used drugs to give him a high he couldn't get any other way, even through his music. In fact, he has said that getting high has helped his musical talents. He also has never made any excuses for his drug use and offers no apologies. But a drug habit is no simple matter, and there were repercussions, of course, as a result of Ray's drug use.

In 1955, Ray and his band were busted in Philadelphia for marijuana possession. They had been sitting in their dressing room after a show. Suddenly the police barged in and took everyone to jail after they found some marijuana in the corner of the room. Ironically, Ray was thought of as a victim. The newspapers blamed his manager, his bandmates, and even his record company! They accused them of forcing Ray to take drugs. This infuriated Ray because it was all wrong. He was responsible for his own habits. He would never lay that rap on someone else.

Playing Music

What Ray has always liked best is to play music. Songs such as "Hallelujah" and "What I Say" made him famous around the country and

Ray Charles often played with
big bands and employed them
on his most popular record,
The Genius of Ray Charles,
released in 1959.

ensured his status as one of the best blues singers in the United States. He was making up to $800 a night by 1959. On any given evening, Ray played jazz, gospel, blues, old-time boogie-woogie, and bebop tunes. There were many styles of music in Ray's repertoire.

In May of 1959, Ray recorded the most popular album of his career. *The Genius of Ray Charles* pulled Ray into the pop music world. On the album, Ray played with big bands and string orchestras. It made him famous around the world.

His talents kept him going all through the 1960s. His albums sold well. People gave him nicknames, such as the High Priest and the Reverend. Atlantic Records called him the Genius. But Ray liked to go by Brother Ray.

Changing Labels

By 1960, Ray had been scratching out a living for fifteen years. Sometimes it was easy, but other times Ray had to struggle. When ABC Records offered him a sweet three-year deal, he couldn't refuse. His star had risen, and he had to go where the money was. He signed with ABC for the high percentage sum of 5 percent royalties on record sales. He also received seven and a half cents on every dollar in profit for being producer on his own albums.

Ray's deal with ABC gave him the chance to travel in comfort and style. Ray purchased a Cessna airplane to fly him and the band to gigs. He began his own record label, named Tangerine after his favorite fruit. Tangerine would oversee the ownership, publishing, and sale of his music. He had constructed a building in Los Angeles to house his company and his own recording studio. Ray had a studio that he could use twenty-four hours a day. No one would ever again tell him the studio was booked, as had happened in the past. The RPM International Building (a building that Ray owned in Los Angeles) was now the hub of Ray Charles Enterprises. Ray was now a businessman as well as a musician.

ABC paid Ray to deliver songs that would be recorded, printed, distributed, and sold by

ABC, but Ray retained ownership of the songs.
Tangerine began to record other artists. Ray had
a lot of responsibility now. These were possibly
his most productive years because he not only
had his own career to handle, but he was also
producing new music.

More Touring and More Albums

Even though Ray wrote less and less of his own
songs, he began to record an album each year.
Recording started in the winter after touring
season had ended. In March and April, his band
toured the South and West. Then they toured
Europe. In August, they returned to the United
States and toured the Northeast. In the fall, they
toured Japan. This is how the band operated for
the next thirty years. Ray decided this was the
best way to stay on top and make the most
money. Business had to be constant in order for
the most profit to be made.

Ray's first ABC album was 1960's *Genius Hits
the Road*. This R & B album featured "Georgia
on My Mind," which hit number one on the

Did You Know?

Ray Charles has won a total of twelve Grammy Awards. In 1960, he won his first Grammy Award; he won four in total. Ray won Best Vocal Performance Album, Male; Best Vocal Performance, Single Record or Track, Male; Best Rhythm and Blues Performance; and Best Performance by a Pop-Single Artist. In 1993, he received his most recent Grammy Award for Best R & B Vocal Performance, Male.

charts and later became the song most associated with Ray.

The next album came later that year. *Dedicated to You* was an album that was all about ladies. And around Christmas, *Genius + Soul = Jazz* hit the stores with a mixture of jazz and R & B. Ray was on fire. In 1962, he recorded his top-selling album, *Modern Sounds in Country and Western.*

What Ray did with, and for, the country and western sounds made America and the world bow at his feet. He was truly a musical genius, and now everyone knew it. "I Can't Stop Loving You" came from this album and happened to be his all-time best-selling and most beloved single.

More Drug Busts

In 1961, at an Indianapolis, Indiana, hotel, Ray woke up to pounding at his door. This was unusual. No one woke Ray unless it was an emergency. He called, "Who's there?" from his bed. "Western Union," was the reply. Ray answered the door in his underwear. Cops poured in and searched the room. This time they found Ray's heroin. Ray was taken to jail.

Newspaper headlines exposed what had been an open secret until then. Ray was a junkie superstar. After a few hours in jail, Ray's road manager and lawyer posted bail. For the time being, Ray was free. He did his concert that night and appeared in court the next morning. A trial was set for a few months away. But Ray had

Attorney Dave Lewis speaks for his client, Ray Charles, after Ray's arrest for possession of heroin in Indianapolis, Indiana in November 1961.

money, and money bought good lawyers. Ray's lawyer saw that the cops hadn't used a warrant to enter his room. They'd fooled Ray into opening the door. The case never went to trial, and the charges were dropped.

In 1965, Ray was arrested again. Circumstances were different this time. His plane had just landed in Boston from Montreal, Canada. Customs officers knew Ray's reputation. They were watching him. Ray went to his hotel, but then realized he'd left his heroin on the plane. He would need it before his show. He and his driver went back to the airport at 5:30 in the morning. Now the customs officers were suspicious. Ray went into the plane with his driver and left after twenty minutes. The customs officers met him outside the plane.

They asked him why he'd come back to the airport. Ray claimed he forgot a book. Then they asked him if he'd mind being searched. Ray minded all right, but he couldn't do anything about it. They searched his coat and found his stash. He was caught red-handed again.

This bust was unlike the others. United States Customs was a federal agency. Ray was

looking at some hard time with this arrest. He
made bail after a few hours and did his Boston
show that night. News hadn't hit the papers or
television yet. But Ray knew it would. This was a
bad situation.

Getting Help

Ray was caught with over three ounces of heroin.
The feds could charge him with smuggling,
possession, and dealing. The only good thing was
that Ray made bail. He could continue playing
his gigs for now. The next year would be tough.
Ray realized he needed to go straight to try and
keep from going to jail. He took 1965 off from
touring and went into rehab.

Ray met with Dr. Frederick Hacker, a well-
known psychiatrist. Dr. Hacker agreed to treat
Ray and then testify for his character. Ray went
cold turkey—he didn't take any drugs to ease
him off his addiction. For a few days, Ray went
through addiction withdrawal. The press got the
news a few weeks later. Ray's contract with ABC
was in jeopardy. If he didn't go to jail, his career
could still be over.

Ray Charles, pictured here during a show in 1971, spent the 1960s and 1970s traveling the world.

After months of treatment, Ray went to Boston for trial. The judge was lenient. With all that Ray had done for himself, and all that he meant as a role model, he was given five years probation. This storm had passed, and Ray had once again survived. He didn't take heroin again after kicking his habit.

World Travel

As always, Ray continued to travel. In the 1960s and 1970s, he traveled to more than fifty countries. Europeans loved the passion of his jazz. The Asian audiences sang along at his concerts. South Americans felt his energy through every note. And America was holding onto its own.

As the years rolled on, his band changed members. Musicians moved on to form their own bands. Ray searched for better sounds. Whatever the lineup, everyone knew that Ray was the boss. He hired and fired his "cats," as he called them. He was equally protective of them, too.

One night in Munich, Germany, he and the band were late getting to their gig. Norman Ganz, the booking agent, was furious and

told the band to get onstage immediately.
Ray told his band to go get dressed. Ganz
exploded. Ray didn't care. He was going to put
on a show, but not in any rushed fashion. The
crowd would wait patiently because they knew
they'd see a good show. And Ray showed
everyone that no one pushed his cats around.

1970s Road Band

Through the 1970s, Ray and his band played halls
both large and small across America and Europe.
But things had changed in music. Tastes had
changed. People were no longer buying the slow
jazz and blues at the rate they had in the '60s. Ray
was unwilling to change. Therefore, his record
sales declined.

He'd left ABC in 1969. His Tangerine record
label released his albums now. He used ABC to
distribute and promote his albums, but Ray was
his own company now. Unfortunately, business
was not good. He made more money producing
other bands than his own. That didn't stop Ray
from touring each and every year.

Everything on tour was done by Ray's rules. He seemed obsessed with time. If his contract stated the show started at 8 PM, Ray walked onstage as the second hand struck the hour. If he wanted the bus to leave at 6 AM, the door would close even if a tardy band member was running to catch up. That cat would have to get to the gig on his own—and he'd better show.

Ray gave authority to his road managers, who seemed to change every few years. They were usually musicians with the band who couldn't cut it onstage anymore. In the '70s, there was Dan Briggs, then former trombone player Fred Murrell, and then former bassist Edgar Willis. Regardless of who they were, the job was the same: Make sure the band got to gigs, that hotels hadn't given away reservations, that contracts were met to the letter.

Ray had a thing for discipline onstage, too. Fines were given to band members who didn't wear a bow tie or whose socks didn't match.

The band traveled to gigs on Ray's own plane and bus. His band numbered more than twenty people, and Ray Charles Enterprises had to get them to gigs. Ray had traded in the Cessna in the mid-1960s for a forty-four-seat, twin-engine Martin 404. Ray bought it for $500,000 from American Airlines. Its interior was custom built, with comfortable seats, a lounge area, and a private room in back for Ray. The plane was nicknamed the Buzzard.

Ray's Rules

Ray changed musicians often. If a cat couldn't keep up, or didn't maintain the sound Ray demanded, he or she was out. He broke people in by seeing if they could follow his lead onstage. Forget the drums or bass, which usually hold a song together through their rhythmic beat. Ray demanded that everyone follow him. Naturally, this was difficult for the drummer, who had to constantly watch Ray's tapping foot or swaying body to find the required beat. This system often led to angry confrontations.

One night the band was playing the Sahara Hotel in Las Vegas. Ray's guitarist, Eugene Ross, had been angry with Ray the whole tour. Ross was

As a bandleader, Ray enforced band discipline without hesitation.

nicknamed Big Bubba because he weighed 400 pounds. Bubba had watched Ray be mean to his band members all through the tour. More and more Ray would yell at people onstage, in front of the audience. Bubba didn't think this was right at all. But no one else backed him up.

That night in Vegas, the band was playing "Busted," a bluesy song that let Ray's voice mellow and groan through lyrics peppered with images of hard times. On cue, Bubba came in with his guitar licks, but the amplifier was set too high. His chords drowned out Ray's vocals. Ray's head swung around and he yelled for Bubba to stop playing. For Bubba, it was the last straw.

The mammoth Texan swore at Ray. He got up and stood his ground. Ray, of course, couldn't see Bubba, but he sensed his presence. The band had stopped playing, and the crowd sat in stunned silence. Ray called through the microphone for someone to take Bubba off the stage. A few of the band members whispered to Bubba, telling him to take it easy. Bubba was in too much of a rage to listen to reason any longer.

Bubba called Ray a dirty dog. Ray tried to laugh it off and told the audience Bubba was drunk. Bubba kept hurling insults. Ray got angry. He screamed for the hall security guards to come get Bubba off the stage. Guards came onstage but stopped before the huge man. Then Clifford Solomon, a saxophonist, got Bubba's attention and pleaded with him. Bubba walked offstage.

Ray immediately called for the band to pick up exactly where the song had left off. They did, and Ray sang, and the audience cheered. Backstage, Bubba had calmed down. He knew he'd just lost his job. Later, Ray didn't seem fazed by the outburst. He even paid Bubba for the rest of the week and paid his way home, too. Bubba had crossed Ray, though, and there was no way Ray was going to let him stay. Many in the band saw Bubba as a hero; he'd been the only one to stand up to Ray like that.

Divorce

After twenty-one years of marriage, Della Bea had had enough. By 1976, Ray had been on the road nine or ten months out of each year they'd known each other. Their three boys had grown into their teens pretty much without having real father-son relationships. Also, Ray's many love affairs had hurt Della Bea to the bottom of her heart.

Still, Ray and Della Bea had a lasting relationship after their divorce. Their three boys were still a part of Ray's life. Della Bea also spoke with Ray from time to time. She asked him for advice or just wanted to hear how he was. They still loved each other. They simply could no longer be husband and wife.

Musical Obscurity

Because Ray wouldn't change his style, he couldn't sell records. Rock and roll, disco, and even pop music had passed him by, it seemed. Listeners wanted fast, loud, and furious music. Ray was all about soul, he has said, and soul came from the heart. Soul played on its own time and in its own manner. But unfortunately, the listening audience didn't agree with Ray's musical philosophy.

By 1977, Ray became a true freelance recording artist. He signed small deals with different record labels. He did a couple of albums for Decca, then went back to Atlantic for two albums. It was no use, though. The songs were old and tired. People were no longer listening to Ray Charles.

The 1980s Comeback

After having lived the traveling life for twenty-five years, Ray finally realized that something had to change for him to remain a popular and successful artist. He needed a new audience. In order to kick start his career, he was going to have to try something new.

Television, Movies, and "String Gigs"

Ray was a regular on television talk shows in the late 1970s. Johnny Carson and Dinah Shore featured him playing solo piano or with a small band on their television shows. Yet he was always playing to an older crowd. It was the same crowd that had followed him twenty years before. But these people weren't buying albums anymore. They were hardly getting out and going to shows, either. What Ray needed was to entice a younger audience. If an older musician could be seen as someone who thought like a young person, acted like a young person, and could have a good time, he'd have a chance to bring that younger audience to his music.

In 1980, Ray appeared in a cameo role as the owner of a music shop in *The Blues Brothers.* The few days he spent filming on the south side of Chicago helped Ray's spirits. He warmed to Dan Akroyd and John Belushi. The movie, of course, became a huge hit, and Ray's sound did make an impression on the movie's younger

Ray poses with Johnny Cash *(center)* during Cash's television special, *Johnny Cash: Spring Fever*. With them are *(left to right)* Waylon Jennings, Jessi Colter, and Johnny Cash's wife, June Carter Cash.

audience. This was the start of the newfound fame that was to come.

In May 1980, Ray began to play concerts with symphony orchestras. He was trying something new after all. He appeared on a PBS special with the Boston Pops orchestra. Ray would use these big "string gigs" as a way of keeping himself in the public eye. They also paid well at $50,000 a performance.

Conquering Nashville

Symphonies, television, and movies had kept Ray in the public eye. But he wanted musical recognition. He actually wanted more than that. He wanted to be on top again, just like he had been during his '60s stardom. Since there was little to prove in the R & B or blues market, Ray set his sights again on country music.

The success Ray had had with *Modern Sounds in Country and Western* back in 1962 had helped him make contacts in Nashville. In 1982, Columbia Records signed Ray to a multialbum deal. His first two albums were OK. There was little spark in his

Did You Know?

Ray Charles has done television commercials for McDonald's (1976) and Pepsi-Cola (1990). His Pepsi spots gave us the catch phrase "You got the right one, baby. Uh-huh."

country variations that gained recognition from the huge country and western audience. Ray was learning country music again, but this time he needed to learn country the Nashville way. It was his only chance to make the smash that he was determined to make in Nashville.

In 1984, Ray chose Nashville producer Billy Sherrill to become his producer, instead of Ray producing his albums himself. Billy had worked with Ray on *Friendship* and had made Tammy Wynette a star when he produced "Stand by Your Man." Tanya Tucker was also one of his great finds for Columbia Records. And he'd helped George Jones make a huge comeback, too. Ray's *Friendship* featured duets with a dozen of country music's finest artists. It was released in 1985 and rose to number one on the country and western charts.

Ray's last country album was released in 1986. *From the Pages of My Mind* was Ray's solo country album. It was again produced by Sherrill and did all right in the music stores. But Ray was antsy and planned to do no more with country music. He'd achieved what he had planned, and now Ray wanted to go back to what he knew best: R & B. He planned a new album with Columbia (his last with that label) for the next year.

More Television

Having given himself a new lease on life, Ray wasn't about to let the new limelight dim. In 1986, he continued his talk-show appearances, playing his R & B classics and "America the Beautiful," his other signature song.

Ray showed up on two television shows in cameo roles that year. In one appearance, he

A Deaf Musician?

In 1983, Ray and his band were touring the country and western clubs in the South. After only a month on the road, Ray began to feel pain in his left ear. When he breathed, he heard hollow swishing sounds. It seemed plugged up. His singing became too loud, as did his normal talking level. Without his hearing, Ray found it difficult walking down hallways or getting around obstacles. Ray tried to ignore it, but after two more months, he began to wonder if he was going deaf. The mere thought frightened him. How could he function deaf if he was already sightless? He needed to see a doctor.

Ray was referred to Dr. Jack Pulec, an ear specialist. After the examination, Dr. Pulec assured Ray that he wasn't going to lose his hearing. It turned out that Ray had a hole in the eustachian tube connected to his eardrum. The sounds he was hearing were called autophony, normal sounds the body made internally that were coming up through the hole in the tube. Dr. Pulec repaired the troubled ear by making an opening in his left eardrum and putting in a tube that allowed the sounds to naturally escape. After a few months, Ray's hearing problems went away. It was one of the scariest moments in the singer's life.

played himself on *Who's the Boss*. Television seemed sweet to Ray. He could really be himself and have fun. The sitcom *Designing Women* used Ray's classic "Georgia on My Mind" as its theme song while the credits played.

Philanthropy

Ray's ear problems in 1983 gave him pause to think about how lucky he was. He knew his money had given him the best medical care available in the world. But he wondered about all those people—and kids—who had the same problem he had had but didn't have the amount of money Ray was fortunate enough to have. They could be deaf.

Ray decided that he wanted to do something for the cause of fighting hearing loss. He talked with his doctor, Dr. Jack Pulec, and discussed creating the Ray Charles Foundation. Ray asked Dr. Pulec questions about the state of medical help for hearing loss. Dr. Pulec told Ray that the cochlear implant needed improvement. Some people believe that profoundly deaf people were

Ray embraces Billy Joel after introducing the younger performer during Joel's induction into the Rock and Roll Hall of Fame in March 1999.

helped most with the cochlear implant. Ray was impressed. He wanted to know how much research would cost to make improvements.

Ray established the foundation that bears his name and gave $250,000 for its first year of operation. He made and kept pledges to continue the fund on a yearly basis.

Awards and Recognition

As an elder statesman of music, Ray had given a lot to the industry, to fans, to charities, and to music history. He began to reap the benefits with awards from many civic groups and music industry organizations.

The most notable recognition from the industry was Ray's induction as a founding member into the Rock and Roll Hall of Fame in 1986. Also on the list of recipients that year were Chuck Berry, Little Richard, and Elvis Presley.

His home state of Florida honored him for his gifts to the arts. They sent him a card in braille. Ray thanked Florida with the words, "It's a wonderful thing to come back to where it all began."

Ray, with Lucille Ball on the left, laughs at jokes made by President Ronald Reagan at a Kennedy Center Honors ceremony in 1986.

On December 8, 1986, Ray received the highest award given to a member of the arts community: the Kennedy Center Honors Medal. The Kennedy Center medal is given by the U.S. government for contributions to the arts. Ray was humbled and wasn't sure he really wanted to go. But of course he had to. He sat through a formal dinner at the United States State Department the Friday before. On Saturday, he appeared at the White House, staying close to his old friend, record producer Quincy Jones. At the main event on Sunday evening, Ray smiled with glee and bathed in the glow of honor. In his honor, children from the Florida School for the Deaf and Blind sang "America the Beautiful." Where Ray was usually embarrassed with such huge affairs, this one was truly special.

After the awards and recognitions for the year had stopped, Ray did what he always did: went back to work.

On Cruise Control

In 1997, Rhino Records made a deal with Ray to put out a five-CD boxed set. *Ray Charles: Genius and Soul* is a 102-song retrospective of Ray's long, successful career. The songs were digitally remastered and put together with more care than ever before.

Pushing Forward

Ray had a ball helping to pick the songs for *Ray Charles: Genius and Soul,* once his seven-figure advance was in the bank. Even while working on this project, he was recording in his studio at night.

Through all the success during the 1960s and then the depressing 1970s, Ray didn't give up. His change in the 1980s was not defensive. Ray was always on the offensive, pushing himself and, at least in his mind, his music forward. And at sixty-seven years old, Ray still had the energy of a young man.

As 2000 came and went, Ray was where it seemed he'd always been: traveling and playing the blues. What had changed in more than fifty years on the road was not the music. Ray was crooning, swinging, and howling the blues as always. He cut an album over the winter, as usual, and by March or April was playing across America. Of course, Europe would come in the fall.

Breaking Through to a Younger Audience

What had changed since the down times of the '70s were Ray's fans. His fans were looking

Ray Charles thrilled audiences at the Hollywood Bowl in Hollywood, California, when he closed the two-day Playboy Jazz Festival in June 1988.

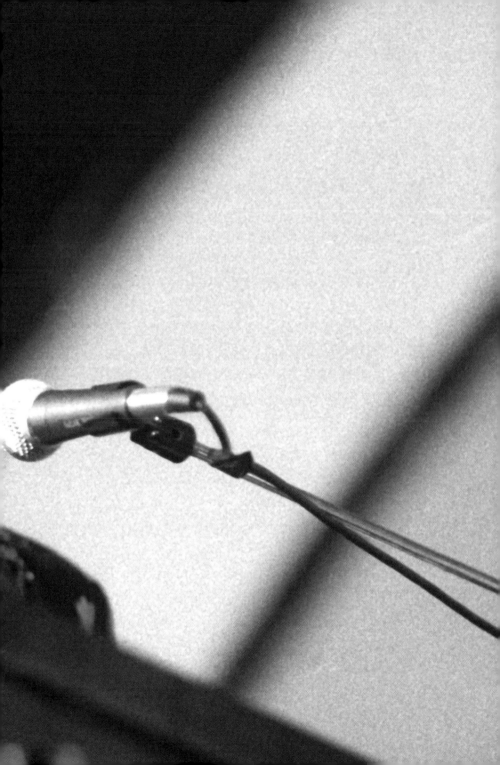

Did You Know?

There's a lot of money today for a good music artist. How long that artist lasts is another story. Most bands break up after two albums. Ray Charles has recorded more than sixty-five albums and is still playing after more than fifty years on the road.

younger. He'd finally broken through as the "old guy" trying to get a new audience. Well, this old guy wasn't simply looking for a new audience. Ray was looking to entertain everyone, including young people.

He hadn't ever quite mastered the method by which he could do this. When the television music channel MTV faxed Ray an invitation to perform on their *Unplugged* series in 1996, the faxes went unanswered. Why? Ray hadn't heard of *Unplugged*. What *Unplugged* did for Tony Bennett's appeal to younger audiences, Ray surely could have achieved. Yet his ignorance made him appear out of touch with the listening audience. This was far from the actual truth.

Ray was in tune with all audiences by way of his musical tastes and talents. Music always moves

Despite changing fads, Ray continues to gain new fans while playing, touring, and creating new music.

forward, but it is also cyclical. The sounds that were happening twenty or thirty years ago have never quite gone away. They only appear in different forms. Ray would tell any fan, "It's in the notes, it's in the rhythm!" "It" is the soul of music. The perfect example is MTV's *Unplugged*. Rock's hardest rockers sit down and play loud music to the crowds in softer tones. The bluesiest bluesmen, jazziest trumpeters, and even '50s and '60s passionate crooners like Tony Bennett, made a splash because, once again, the message was in the music, not in the volume. And this is exactly what Ray has known all along.

Dozens of interviewers have asked Ray what "soul" is. Ray's answer would often begin with a laugh or a chuckle. From behind his dark glasses, this man of genius has a vision uncommon to us all. The fact that he can't actually see doesn't mean a thing. He has said, "[Soul is] the feeling that comes through in the music. That's the essence of soul. The words tell you that."

SELECTED DISCOGRAPHY

1957 *Ray Charles* (also known as *Hallelujah I Love Her So*)

1958 *Ray Charles at Newport*

1959 *The Genius of Ray Charles*

1960 *Ray Charles in Person*

1961 *Genius + Soul = Jazz*

1962 *Modern Sounds in Country and Western Music*

1963 *Ingredients in a Recipe for Soul*

1964 *Have a Smile with Me*

1966 *Ray's Moods*

1969 *I'm All Yours, Baby*

1970 *Love Country Style*

1972 *Through the Eyes of Love*

1974 *Come Live with Me*

1977 *True to Life*

1979 *Ain't It So*

1984 *Friendship*

1993 *My World*

1998 *Dedicated to You*

2000 *Sittin' on Top of the World*

GLOSSARY

bebop A type of music from the 1950s that uses a two-beat rhythm.

big band Musical group of between eight and over twenty musicians, popular from the 1940s into the early 1960s.

blues A type of jazz that has a slow tempo, developed in the American South.

boogie-woogie A kind of jazz that repeats musical rhythms.

braille A system of writing, invented by Frenchman Louis Braille, that uses raised dots on a page for letters to help blind people read.

gig A music concert.

glaucoma An eye disease that causes blindness.

heroin A powerful and illegal narcotic.

innovation A way of changing something, like the way music is played, that is pleasing to many people.

jazz A musical style invented by black

Americans in the early 1900s in New Orleans, which uses upbeat tempos in songs that has solo parts for each instrument.

junkie A slang term used to describe a person who is addicted to heroin.

matriarch The female leader of a family or group of people; a person who has a lot of knowledge.

R & B (rhythm and blues) A type of music developed by black Americans in the 1940s that combines blues and jazz.

style In music, the way a musician plays an instrument or sings.

swing A type of music that was played mostly by big bands in the 1930s and that is dance-based with rapid rhythms.

union A group of people who work together for better wages and treatment from employers.

version A different way of doing something.

Memphis Rock 'N' Soul Museum
145 Lt. George W. Lee Avenue
Memphis, TN 38103
(901) 543-0800
Web site: http://www.memphisrocknsoul.org

Ray Charles Fan Club
RCR Production
Attn: Raenee Robinson
2107 West Washington Boulevard, Suite 200
Los Angeles, CA 90018
Web site: http://www.raycharles.com/fanclub.htm

Rock and Roll Hall of Fame and Museum
One Key Plaza
Cleveland, OH 44144
(888) 764-ROCK (7625)
Web site: http://www.rockhall.com

Web Sites

Due to the changing nature of Internet links, the Rosen Publishing Group, Inc., has developed an online list of Web sites related to the subject of this book. This site is updated regularly. Please use this link to access the list:

http://www.rosenlinks.com/rrhf/rcha/

FOR FURTHER READING

Bell, Sharon, and George Ford Mathis. *Ray Charles.* New York: Lee & Low Books, 2001.

Gribin, Anthony J., et al. *The Complete Book of Doo-Wop.* Iola, WI: Krause Publications, 2000.

Ritz, David. *Ray Charles: Voice of Soul.* Philadelphia: Chelsea House, 1994.

Rosalsky, Mitch. *Encyclopedia of Rhythm and Blues and Doo Wop Vocal Groups.* Lanham, MD: Scarecrow Press, 2000.

Turk, Ruth. *Ray Charles: Soulman.* Minneapolis: The Lerner Publishing Group, 1996.

Works Cited

Charles, Ray, and David Ritz. *Brother Ray.* New York: Warner, 1978.

Lydon, Michael. *Ray Charles: Man and Music.* New York: Penguin, 1998.

INDEX

A

ABC Records, 64–66, 71, 74
"America the Beautiful," 88, 95
Anderson, Joe (musician), 37–38
Atlantic Records, 54, 55, 64, 81

B

"Baby, Let Me Hold Your
      Hand," 47
Bell, Johnny (musician), 55
Billy Shaw Agency, 53–54
Blues Brothers, The, 83–86
Brantley, Charlie (musician), 41
Bridgewater, Joe (musician), 55
Briggs, Dan (road manager), 75
Brother Ray (autobiography), 8,
      9, 38
Brown, Charles, 33, 36, 41, 45, 51
"Busted," 78

C

Charles, Ray
    with ABC Records, 64–66,
       71, 74
    with Atlantic Records, 54–55,
       64, 81
    awards and recognition,
       93–95
    and blindness, 5, 11, 12,
       14–20, 21, 28
    childhood of, 7–23
    children of, 50–51, 59, 60, 80
    with Columbia Records,
       86–87, 88
    comeback, 82–88
    drug use/drug busts, 60–61,
       68–73
    early records, 46–47, 54
    health problems, 71, 89–90, 91
    and his band, 54–57, 73–79
    interest in music as child, 6,
       11–13, 19–20, 21–22
    in Jacksonville, FL, 26–36
    living with Thompson family,
       26–27, 34–35
    in Los Angeles, 50–53
    marriages/relationships with
       women, 35–36, 42–43, 44,
       47–50, 53, 59, 60, 79–80
    in McSon Trio, 46–47, 50, 51
    in Nashville, TN, 86–87
    in Orlando, FL, 36–38
    and philanthropy, 91–93
    on the road, 23, 53–54, 55,
       59, 66, 73–76, 89, 97
    in Rock and Roll Hall of
       Fame, 93
    in Seattle, WA, 44–50, 60
    and success/lack of,
       65–66, 76, 80–81

in Tampa, FL, 39–43
and Tangerine record label,
    65, 66, 74
television and movies, 83–86,
    88–91
writing music, 37–38, 51–53
and younger audiences,
    97–101
Cole, Nat King, 33, 35, 36, 41, 51
Columbia Records, 86–87, 88
"Confession Blues," 46

D

Decca record label, 81
Dedicated to You, 67
Downbeat Records, 46

E

Ertegun, Ahmet (Atlantic
    Records), 55

F

Florida Playboys, 41–42
Freddie and Lydia (sisters in
    Tampa, FL), 41, 42
Friendship, 87, 88
From the Pages of My Mind, 88
Fulson, Lowell (musician), 51–53

G

Ganz, Norman (booking agent),
    73–74
Garred, Milt (musician), 46
Genius Hits the Road, 66
Genius of Ray Charles, The, 64

Genius + Soul = Jazz, 67
"Georgia on My Mind," 66–67, 91
Grand Ole Opry, 34

H

Hacker, Dr. Frederick, 71
"Hallelujah," 61
Herman, Lovie (girlfriend), 35–36
Howard, Della Bea (wife), 59–60,
    79–80

I

"I Can't Stop Loving You," 68
"I Found My Baby There," 42
"I Got a Woman," 57

J

Jones, Quincy (musician), 95

L

Lauderdale, Jack (Downbeat
    Records), 46, 50, 51
Louise (friend of Mary Jane
    Robinson), 26–27

M

Ma Beck (matriarch of
    Greenville), 22–23
McGee, Gosady (musician), 41, 46
McSon Trio, 46–47, 50, 51
Miller, Johnny (musician), 47
Mitchell, Louise (girlfriend),
    42–43, 44, 47–51
*Modern Sounds in Country and
    Western*, 67–68, 86
Moore, Oscar and Johnny, 47

Murrell, Fred (road manager), 75

N

Newman, David "Fathead," 54
Norris, A. D., 55

P

Peoples, Bill (musician), 55
Pitman, Georgia ("Miss Georgia"), 12, 22
Pitman, Wylie ("Mr. Pit"), 11–13, 19, 22
Pulec, Dr. Jack, 89–90, 91

R

Raeletts (backup singers), 55–57
Ray Charles Enterprises, 65, 75–76
Ray Charles Foundation, 91–93
Ray Charles: Genius and Soul, 96–97
Red Wing Cafe (Greenville, FL), 11–13, 19
Rhino Records, 96
Robinson, Bailey (father), 7–9
Robinson, David (son), 60
Robinson, Evelyn (daughter), 50–51
Robinson, George (brother), 8, 10–11
    death of, 13–14
Robinson, Mary Jane (wife of Bailey), 8–9, 22, 26
Robinson, Ray Jr. (son), 59
Robinson, Robert (son), 60
Rock and Roll Hall of Fame, 93

Ross, Eugene "Big Bubba" (musician), 76–79
RPM International Building, 65

S

Sherrill, Billy (producer), 87–88
Solomon, Clifford (musician), 79
State School for the Blind (St. Augustine, FL), 16, 17–19, 26
"Sun's Gonna Shine Again, The," 54
Sunshine Club (Orlando, FL), 37

T

Tangerine record label, 65, 66, 74
Thompson, Fred, 26–27, 34–35
Thompson, Lena Mae, 26–27, 34–35

U

Unplugged (MTV), 100–102

W

Washington, Henry (musician), 32
"What I Say," 61
White, Clanky (musician), 55
Williams, Aretha (mother), 7–11, 13–14, 16–17, 37
    death of, 22–23
Williams, Eileen (wife), 53
Willis, Edgar (road manager), 75

Y

York, Tiny (musician), 36

About the Author

Mark Beyer has written on subjects as varied as military hardware and life in the future. His interest in biographies stems from his passion for education. He lives outside New York City.

Photo Credits

Cover, pp. 4, 5, 7, 10, 30–31, 40, 58, 69, 72, 77, 82, 94, 96, 98–99, 101 © Corbis; pp. 15, 92 © AP/Wide World Photos; pp. 26, 34, 62–63, 84–85 © Hulton/Archive/Getty Images; pp. 44, 48–49, 52, 56 © Michaels Ochs Archive.

Editor

Eliza Berkowitz

Series Design

Tom Forget

Layout

Nelson Sá